Become an Ocean Champion!

Pamela Jackson

D1164803

Mary Ann Goodrich
13825 Mira Montana Dr.
Del Mar, Ca. 92014

This book belongs to

MARY ANN GOODRICH

My Ocean Pledge

I promise to learn all I can about the oceans and the animals living there and to become an ocean champion.

Signed: _____

Ocean Adventures
With Jax

by Pamela Jackson
Illustrated by Bonnie Bright

Everything Oceans®

Ocean Adventures With Jax
by Pamela Jackson
Illustrated by Bonnie Bright
Edited by Lise Strom, B.A., M.A.

Published by EverythingOceans, Inc.

www.EverythingOceans.com

Text and illustrations copyright © 2016 EverythingOceans, Inc.

All rights reserved.
No part of this book may be reproduced or used
in any form by any means without permission in
writing from EverythingOceans, Inc.

Library of Congress Control Number: 2015956234

ISBN: 978-0-9904169-4-4

Hi! I'm Sparkle the Sea Star. Be sure to
check out my glossary of fun ocean words
at the back of the book.

Dedications

*To the children of the world who feel empowered to make a difference:
May we work together to protect the oceans and the animals that live
there. To my husband, David, for always believing in me;
you are the wind beneath my wings.*
~Pamela Jackson

Thank you, Mom and Dad, for providing me with a childhood filled
with trips to the beach and exploring the ocean, and for
supporting my dreams of becoming an illustrator.
~Bonnie Bright

Where will the oceans take me today? My name is Jax. I'm a bottlenose dolphin. Come dive into my world. Ready, set, go!

I'm gonna splash you!

My **dolphin** family and friends are called a **pod**. We're **mammals**, just like you. This means we're warm blooded and breathe air, except we live in the ocean! We love to play and explore. I'm on my way with my friends to our favorite playground, an old shipwreck.

We already found this cool compass there. Today we're searching for more things to add to our collection. What do you think we'll find?

On our way to the shipwreck we jump, twirl, splish-splash in the waves, and blow bubbles with our **blowholes**.

A **blowhole** is a nostril; a breathing hole on top of our head! We have fun playing pass the **seaweed** with our flippers.

YIPPY!!!

Dolphins have our own special way of talking called **echolocation**. We make clicks, whistles, and squeaks. These sounds bounce off objects under water and come back to us as a picture made out of sound. Our special power of **echolocation** gives us lots of information. It helps us find food, find our way around the ocean, and keep in touch with our **pod**.

When we arrive at the shipwreck,
I see something shiny in the sand.
Do you see what it is? Maybe I
should use my **rostrum**, my snout,
to dig it out!

Do you see something else? Yikes! There's a **shark**! Gulp! When I turn around, my friends are gone.

I wonder which way they went? I'd better get out of here.

SWOOSH!!!

I swim this way, but it just gets deeper and colder. I swim that way and it just gets darker. It's no use. When I finally stop swimming, I'm lost. Uh-oh! I should have listened to my mom. She said I should stay close to my **pod**, pay attention to where I am, and ask for help if I get lost.

I'll use my **echolocation** power to call for help.
Click, whistle, whistle, click, squeak. Click,
whistle, whistle, click, squeak. Hey! There's
a big eye staring at me. I'm scared.

A deep, soothing voice says, "My name is Fluke. Did you call me? I'm a **humpback whale**. I'm one of the largest animals on the planet and I eat some of the smallest—**krill**. Don't be afraid."

"Jumping **jellyfish**! You're huge! Mom says whales are kind and wise. I'm glad I found you. My name is Jax. Can you please help me find my **pod**?"

"Yes, of course I'll help you."

"Fluke, what are those big fish zipping by?"

"Those are **bluefin tuna** and they're **endangered**."

"What does **endangered** mean?"

"It means they are <u>in</u> <u>danger</u> and need special protection."

"Now it's late and getting dark. You need to return to your **pod** where you'll be safe. Our ocean home is a beautiful place, but it has dangers too, like that **shark** you saw. Let's swim along together."

Soon we find the **coral reef** near my home. **Corals** are tiny animals that grow together in warm waters to make a reef. Corals come in many beautiful colors.

Fluke and I hear the familiar clicks, whistles, and squeaks of my dolphin **pod**. It feels good to be back home!

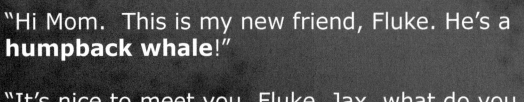

"Hi Mom. This is my new friend, Fluke. He's a **humpback whale**!"

"It's nice to meet you, Fluke. Jax, what do you say?"

"Thanks, Fluke, for becoming my friend and helping me find my way home."

"Jax, where have you been?"

"Ummm, well, I got lost because my friends and I went treasure hunting today. Look what I found to add to our collection!"

"I see you're excited about the golden key, we'll look at it later. I've been very worried about you."

"I know, but mom..."

"No buts. What rules are you supposed to remember?"

"I know: Stay close to my **pod**, pay attention to my surroundings, and call for help if I get lost. Mom! I did call for help and a **humpback whale** heard me! I'm getting better at using **echolocation**."

"Ok Jax, you are getting better at **echolocation**. You found Fluke to help you come home. But, next time, remember rule #1. Now eat your yummy fish and squid dinner. Then it's off to sleep!"

"Will you tell me a pirate or a mermaid story?"

"Alright. Once upon a time when the oceans were beautiful and clean..."

Later, while drifting off to sleep, I think about my
new friend Fluke and the **endangered
blue fin tuna**. I hope I'll
see them again soon.

"G'night Mom, I love you."

"I love you too, Jax.
Sweet reef-dreams."

I wonder what this key is for? I can't wait to find out on my next adventure! I hope you'll join me.

Sparkle's Glossary

BLOWHOLE
A breathing hole or nostril on top of a dolphin or whale's head that allows it to breathe air at the surface of the water.

BLUEFIN TUNA (Endangered)
A very large fish that is blue on top, silver on the bottom, and lives in the open ocean. Unlike other fish, tuna are warm blooded and among the ocean's fastest swimmers, reaching speeds of 30 miles per hour. They typically grow to about 6 feet in length and weigh about 300 pounds.

BOTTLENOSE DOLPHIN
A marine mammal with a dorsal fin, long body, and cone shaped teeth. Dolphins breathe air with their lungs. They use echolocation to find food, find their way, and to communicate with their pod.

Bottlenose dolphins are very adaptable and are found in all oceans of the world except the Arctic and Antarctic. They are active hunters that eat a wide variety of fishes, squids, crabs, and shrimp.

Dolphins sleep, but unlike people, they sleep with only half of their brain at a time. One half stays awake to protect the animal from dangers and to remember to breathe. Dolphins can switch which side of their brain is asleep so both sides of their brain get to rest.

CORAL REEF
A collection of tiny animals living in the shallow, warm waters of oceans. They grow together to build a living structure.

ECHOLOCATION (EH-CO-LOH-KAY-SHUN)
Dolphins use distinct sounds like clicks, whistles, and squeaks to communicate. They receive returning sound waves to identify the size and location of objects, find food, and explore their ocean world.

ENDANGERED
An endangered animal is one of only a few of its kind left in the world. Endangered species are placed on a special watch list to protect them from harm. People worry that endangered animals might all die out and become extinct.

HUMPBACK WHALE (Endangered)
One of the largest marine mammals. Humpback whales live in all the oceans of the world. They have the longest migration of any mammal. Whales have huge pectoral fins and grow up to 52 feet in length, about the size of a school bus. They weigh 30 or more tons.

JELLYFISH
A water-filled floating marine animal with tentacles that drifts in the ocean currents. Sometimes plastic bags look just like jellyfish and confuse marine life. Animals can be harmed if they become entangled in the bags or swallow them.

KRILL
Small shrimplike animals (about the size of a paperclip) living in large groups called swarms. Many whales, seals, penguins, squid, and fish eat krill.

MAMMAL
A warm-blooded animal living on land or in the sea. Mammals have hair and a backbone. They give birth to live young (babies) and feed them milk from the mother's body.

POD
A social group (family and friends) of dolphins or whales who swim closely together. A pod's average size is around 10-12 individuals but can be larger.

ROSTRUM (ROS-TRUM)
A dolphin's snout has many uses including digging up food. A rostrum is very hard and can be used as a weapon against predators. Dolphins can ram sharks with enough force to injure or kill them.

SEAWEED
An aquatic plant growing in the ocean. Kelp is a type of seaweed that can grow up to two feet a day.

SHARK
A "torpedo" shaped fish with a dorsal fin. Most sharks have rows of razor sharp teeth that continue to grow throughout their lives. Shark teeth start growing from the back row, forcing the teeth in the front row to fall out. They can lose thousands of teeth in their lifetime. Sharks can detect one drop of blood in a million drops of water. They also have good eyesight and see in color.

Critical Thinking Teacher & Parent Guide

Can You Answer These Questions?

1. What is the main idea of this story?

2. What is a mammal?

3. What smart decisions does Jax make?

4. Can you find five or more things that do not belong in a beautiful and clean ocean? How do you think they got there?

5. What 3 rules does Mom teach Jax? Why are they important?

6. What does endangered mean?

7. What is a blowhole?

8. What is echolocation? Why does Jax use it?

9. What are 3 things we have in common with dolphins?

10. What do you think the key is for?

Attention Parents and Teachers

Visit **www.OceanKids.com** to download complementary coloring pages from your home computer. Also available for purchase is a companion guide to support your child's learning.

About the Author

Pamela Jackson was born with gills. Well, not really, but given the depth of her love for all things under the sea, she might as well have been. Pamela is a professional Aquarist, children's book author, and Head Content Developer for the internationally acclaimed EverythingOceans® social media campaign. Pamela's life mission is to inspire and equip the next generation to become powerful ocean champions.

Known for her unparalleled ability to demystify the animals that call the ocean home, Pamela's love affair with aquatic life began when she was just five years old. While other little girls took their dolls wherever they went, Pamela took Goldie, the goldfish she won at the state fair. Fast forward a few years and Pamela's home practically transformed into an underwater reef—complete with various salt water tanks and countless ocean species. Pamela went on to graduate with honors from the esteemed Aquarium and Aquaculture Science Program at Saddleback College in California and quickly became known as a distinguished marine life educator. Today, she's a sought-after speaker who partners with parents and teachers worldwide in educating children about ocean life and the importance of ocean conservation.

Pamela lives steps away from the ocean in Southern California and enjoys watching pods of dolphins and whales swim in their natural environment from her living room with her husband, David.

Special thanks to my parents, Sharlene and Malvin, my brother, Shai, and Julie Springer Anderson, my mentor and friend.

About the Illustrator

Bonnie Bright is a professional illustrator of children's books with over sixteen years experience in her craft. She is well recognized for her amazing illustrations and animation of digital books, and was previously an art director, game artist, and animator during a 15–year educational computer game career. Bonnie's expertise includes 3D artwork and animation for major movie websites, such as *Shrek* and *Kung-fu Panda*. Her illustrated books include *The Tangle Tower*, *Surf Angel*, *Denny's Pets*, *Jenny's Pets*, *Cellphoneitus* and *I Love You All the Time*.

In addition to her career as an illustrator, Bonnie runs a beach volleyball club and works in her organic garden. Her website is www.BrightIllustration.com.

EverythingOceans thanks its advisors for their expertise:
Rochelle McReynolds, M.A., B.F.A., Consultant.
Lisa Torbenson, B.A. Education Specialist.

Additional thanks:
Aubrey Rigg Ashford, Bob Godlasky, Gaines Hill, Carolyn Hopkins, Jim Kempton, Carin Latino, Allison Maslan, Stephanie Nivinskus, Janica Smith, Steve Thompson and Christopher Willemse.

Everything Oceans®

About EverythingOceans®

EverythingOceans is a marine life education company that engages, educates, and empowers its global community to become active ocean champions.

EverythingOceans is dedicated to creating experiential content that illuminates life under the sea. The enterprise consists of an educational children's book series, an extensive online ocean directory, and a captivating, robust video series including hands-on learning activities to develop the ocean ambassador in all of us. Passionate, committed and connected with a large and growing audience, EverythingOceans is a compelling voice for inhabitants of the sea.

Children, parents, teachers, and ocean enthusiasts alike rely on EverythingOceans to bring the ocean to life for those of us who cannot see what lies beneath the surface. We invite you to join our community and to play your part in caring for the ocean and our friends living in it.

To Learn More, Visit EverythingOceans.com

CPSIA information can be obtained
at www.ICGtesting.com
Printed in the USA
LVOW06*1159120217
523989LV00008B/10/P

9 780990 416944